Henry and Melinda Sports Stories

THE B STREET FIVE

By Silky Sullivan

Illustrations by Lois Axeman

CHILDRENS PRESS, CHICAGO

For the real Henry and Linda

Library of Congress Cataloging in Publication Data

Sullivan, Silky.
The B Street five.

(Henry and Melinda sports stories)
Summary: Melinda helps the B Street 5 beat the Kings at a basketball game, even though the Kings think that she is a boy.
[1. Basketball—Fiction. 2. Sex role—Fiction] I. Axeman, Lois, ill. II. Title. III. Series: Sullivan, Silky. Henry and Melinda sports stories.
PZ7.S9537Bac [Fic] 81-38468
ISBN 0-516-01918-X AACR2

1 2 3 4 5 6 7 8 9 10 R 91 90 89 88 87 86 85 84 83 82

More than anything else, Henry and Melinda loved to play ball. They had a baseball and a bat. They had a basketball and a net.

Best of all, they had three friends to play with.

T. J., C. J., and P. J. Harvey lived on B Street with Henry and Melinda.

T. J. was the tallest.

C. J. was the smartest.

P. J. was the youngest.

Every afternoon, they came over to play basketball.

One day, C. J. said, "I have an idea. Let's all be one team. Then we can join the games at City Park."

"That sounds like fun," said Henry. "Let's do it."

"First, we need a name," said C. J.

They tried and tried to think of a name. The Nets, the Jets, the Shooting Stars, nothing seemed to fit.

"I know," said Henry. "There are five of us and we live on B Street. Let's call ourselves the B St. 5!"

Everyone liked that name. Melinda brought out her paints. C. J. painted B St. 5 on their shirts.

Then they went to City Park. On the way, they sang this song:

"We are the B St. 5!
No one can beat us,
dead or alive.
We are rough,
We are tough,
We are the B St. 5!
Hurray!"

When they got to City Park, they saw nothing but boys. Boys running, jumping. Boys shooting, shouting. It was very noisy.

Melinda asked, "Where are the girls?"

B st.
5
B st.
5
B st
5

"What?" said Henry.

Melinda asked louder, "Where are the girls?"

"I can't hear you," said Henry.

Melinda shouted, "Where are the girls!"

Everyone turned and stared at them.

"Uh-oh," said C. J. "I think they heard you."

"Man, who's looking for girls?" A tall boy came over. "Ain't no girls around here."

Someone whispered, "That's Long Sam and the Kings. They beat everybody!"

Melinda was not afraid of Long Sam. "What's wrong with girls?"

"Girls are silly."

"They are not," said Melinda. "I am a—!"
P. J. put his hand over her mouth.
"—gmmph!" said Melinda.

Long Sam looked at Henry. "Is this your team?"

Henry nodded. "Sure is."

"Is this little dude with the big mouth any good?"

Henry nodded. "Sure is."

Long Sam looked at Melinda again. "That's cool." He walked away.

"Whew!" said C. J. "That was close."

"He thinks I'm a boy!" cried Melinda.

"I've got news for you," said C. J. "Until we get out of here, you are a boy."

"I don't want to be a boy!"

"You want to get us in trouble?"

"We are in trouble," said Henry. "Those Kings look like they belong in jail."

A big man came over. "I'm in charge of the playground," he said. "The rules are simple. You take turns. Winners keep the court. Cause trouble and I throw you out."

"Thank you," said Henry.

"They play rough," said the man. "That kid is too small."

Henry took her hand. "Do you want to go home?"

"No," said Melinda. "I want to play Long Sam."

The big man went away.

They waited. Team after team lost to the Kings. "I'm scared," said P. J.

"Don't be," said Henry.

"Those Kings are older," said P. J. "And Long Sam is awfully good."

"We'll be all right," said Henry.

At last, it was their turn. The Kings laughed when they saw Melinda.

"You call that a player? Get him a ladder! Put him on stilts!"

Long Sam winked at her.

They played for a long time. The Kings scored. So did the B St. 5. The Kings scored again. So did the B St. 5.

Then Melinda got the ball. She dribbled fast. The Kings could not stop her.

She yelled to Henry, "Run to the basket!" She threw him the ball.

He scored.

The Kings were behind. They did not like that at all.

Melinda got the ball again. The Kings waited for her. She dribbled fast. They tripped her. She did it again. They shoved her down.

"Time out," said Long Sam. He stared at the Kings. "The little dude is good," he said. "Don't push him around."

After that, the Kings played fairly.

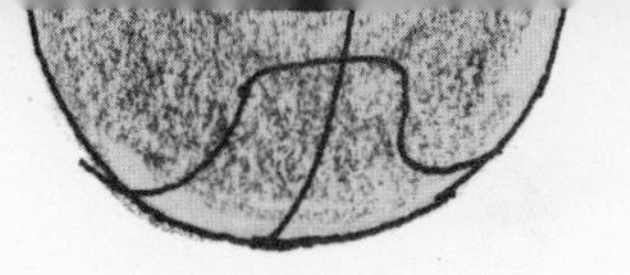

The score was tied again.

Melinda threw the ball to Henry. He threw it back. "Shoot!" he said.

Melinda was surprised.

"Shoot!" said the Harvey brothers. "Hurry!"

Melinda threw the ball with all her might. Whoosh! It slid through the net. It did not touch the rim.

The B St. 5 had won!

Everyone cheered. Long Sam shook hands with Henry. "That was a good game," he said. He winked at Melinda. "Little dude, would you like to be a King?"

"I'm too silly," said Melinda. "I'm a girl."

Long Sam laughed and laughed. “I thought so,” he said. “Too much!” He showed her a fancy way to slap hands. “Little dude, you can be on my team, anytime!”

The B St. 5 went home. On the way, they sang their song:

"We are the B St. 5!
No one can beat us,
dead or alive.
We are rough,
We are tough,
We are the B St. 5!
Hurray!"

UNFAMILIAR WORDS
(based on the Spache Readability Formula)

Most of the following unfamiliar words in *The B Street Five* are made clear through the illustrations and content.

ain't
alive
anytime
awfully
baseball
basketball
bat
charge
cheered
court
dead
dribbled
dude
everybody
everyone
fancy
fit
hurray
I've
jail
kid
net
nets
noisy
ourselves
playground
rim
rough
score
scored
shirts
shout
shouted
shouting
shoved
simple
slap
someone
stared
stilts
tough
trouble
we'll
whew
whoosh
winners
won

About the Author

Silky Sullivan is a Phi Beta Kappa graduate of the University of Michigan and a children's librarian who resides in Royal Oak, Michigan, with her artist husband and their tailless cat. The Henry and Melinda stories were inspired by her husband, who, at age fifteen, began teaching his younger sister, then three, to play basketball. His sister went on to become a superstar and very successful coach. Says Ms. Sullivan, "The whole family loves sports. We're all athletic. I'm writing from experience."

About the Artist

Lois Axeman is a native Chicagoan who lives with her Shih-tzu dog, Marty, in a sunny, plant-filled highrise overlooking a large Chicago park. Marty accompanies Lois to and from her studio in town. After attending the American Academy and the Institute of Design (IIT), Lois started as a fashion illustrator in a department store. When the children's wear illustrator became ill, Lois took her place and found that she loved drawing children. She started freelancing then, and has been doing text and picture books ever since. Lois teaches classes on illustration at the University of Illinois, Circle Campus.